CUPID'S SECOND CHANCE

RETURN TO CUPID, TEXAS #8

SYLVIA MCDANIEL

VIRTUAL BOOKSELLER, LLC

❀ Created with Vellum

Return to Cupid, Texas
Cupid Stupid
Cupid Scores
Cupid's Dance
Cupid Help Me!
Cupid Cures
**Cupid's Heart
Cupid Santa
**Cupid Second Chance
Cupid Charmer
Cupid Crazy
Cupid's Bachelorette
Cupid Games
Return to Cupid Box Set Books 1-3
Cupid Help Me Box Set Books 4-6
**The Unlucky Bride

Want to learn about my new releases before anyone else? Sign up for my New Book Alert and receive a free book.

One Blind Date Too Many

Vanessa Lowell hates Valentine's Day. After her husband was killed in Afghanistan, it's the loneliest day of the year. A reminder of everything she's lost. Unaware that her good friends are setting her up for another blind date, she goes to a party only to meet Disco Dave —yet another bad date.

Three years after the death of his wife, David Baker is tired of his well-meaning friends setting him up. So he becomes Disco Dave, the worst date ever. When he meets Vanessa, he's attracted, but fearful. Cupid has a target on Dave's back and before he can do the Hustle out the door, he's been struck.

Will David and Vanessa put an end to bad dates or do their hearts still belong to their first loves? When you've experienced great love is it possible to love again?

Receive a complimentary book when you sign up for my new book alerts at www.SylviaMcDaniel.com

CHAPTER 1

*V*anessa had spent Christmas alone. Several people invited her to have lunch with them, but she refused. Today, her grief rode her hard, like a wild bucking horse jerking her in every direction. While others were joyous, she experienced utter sadness.

Tonight, she walked through the park with a single rose in her hand. Something urged her to go the statue, so she reacted to her instincts.

A cloud crossed over the moon as she neared the monument, gazing up at the boy in a diaper, she sighed. No one in town realized that her husband was the great-great-great nephew of the famous Thomas Cupid. For this reason, she must've felt compelled to be here.

"Oh, honey, I miss you so much. How can I go on without you?" she said, trying to stop the tears that had flowed all day. As she laid the flower at the foot of Cupid, a shimmering light appeared before her and a warmth filled her.

Rising, she saw the apparition. Her heart stopped for a moment at the image of Kevin, just the way she remembered him. There was no fear, only an outpouring of love.

"Merry Christmas, Vanessa."

The love of her life moved toward her and her husband's lips were on hers once more. As she basked in his embrace, a healing contentment overcame her.

Slowly he released her. "You'll always be my girl, but it's time for us each to move on. Remember our love but live your life to the fullest. Fall in love again, get married, and have those babies you want so badly. I'll always love you but know that I am at peace."

She reached up and touched his face, her fingers caressing his strong jaw once more. "Vaya con Dios, my love. You live on in my heart."

"Goodbye, Vanessa." The sparkling apparition slowly dissipated and she knew he was gone.

"Goodbye, my love," she whispered, her voice cracking.

The sound of Christmas carols resounded in the street, her favorite carol. And she knew it was his way of saying farewell.

Until tonight, they never had the chance to say goodbye. With a sigh, she turned to walk home.

A man stood staring at the statue and she wondered if he'd witnessed the reunion with her husband.

"Is the superstition true?" he asked as she passed.

Stopping, she stared at the statue thinking there must be something magical about the God of Love. "Yes. If you want to meet the love of your life, dance naked around Cupid at midnight."

"Will you be there?" the man asked.

Shaking her head, she smiled. "Not yet. But some day. Merry Christmas."

With a lightness in her heart she hadn't felt in a long time, she continued walking out of the park. Someday, love would find her again. Someday, when she was ready.

CHAPTER 2

A Year Later

Vanessa hated Valentine's Day with a passion. Especially since she had no one to share the day with. Store shelves were lined with candy, cards, and flowers to express love. The day for lovers was like a slap in the face to those who had loved and lost.

Gradually the grief from her husband's death had eased, though not a day went by that she didn't think of him. Sure, she understood he was gone, never to return, and he'd given her his blessing to move on with her life. But a great love didn't just land in your lap. And she was holding out for someone special.

This year for the first time ever, she had done online dating, but out of her three dates, not a one would she see again.

Yes, they were bad.

Tonight, her friends invited her to attend a party celebrating the night they all danced around the Cupid statue and found love. Spending time with a group of couples commemorating when they met was not exactly her first choice of things to do, but she would make an appearance. Three days from now, on Valentine's Day, she planned on hibernating until things returned to normal.

Turning down the lane, she saw the ranch house where Shadow and Jim Lawrence lived. Over a year ago while working at a Christmas event with Brie, she met the Lawrence women and became friends. Today was their way of observing Valentine's with their husbands and children.

A quick appearance and she would be out the door and heading back home.

Parking her car, she noticed all the vehicles. Looked like a large turnout.

Walking up to the door, nerves gripped her stomach. A couple's party, which she still found almost impossible to attend. Hopefully, she would be gone faster than Cupid could pull back his arrow.

When she reached the door, a man stepped up at the same time. He smiled, dimples creasing his cheeks, a trimmed beard covered his jaw, the hair dark and matching what covered his head. His emerald eyes twinkled and brought a smile to her face. The wind whipped around the entryway and she pushed her auburn hair out of her face.

"Hi," he said.

"Hi." For a second, she thought she'd seen him somewhere, but couldn't quite place him.

"If this is a couple's party I'm out of here in five minutes," he said standing on the doorstep.

Turning toward him, she grinned. "My thoughts exactly. Do I know you?"

"No," he said. "David Baker."

"Vanessa Lowell," she said, shaking his outstretched hand. "Nice to meet you."

The attractive man had buff arms, a nice smile, and probably was a serial killer or something if he was single. All she had dated since her husband's untimely death had been one loser after another.

Glancing at the door and then at her shyly, he pressed the bell. "Here we go."

Jim opened the door. "David and Vanessa, so glad you came. Come on in."

Strolling through the entryway, Vanessa glanced at all the Valentine decorations. "Wow. Did you buy the store out of paper Cupids and hearts?"

The house looked like someone had exploded in the room with hearts, cupids, and tinsel. They were definitely into Valentine's Day.

Jim laughed. "My wife went a little overboard. We are

together because of a bet I lost that had me dancing naked around Cupid in the town square. Let me take your coats and then you guys mingle and say hello to everyone." He paused. "Have the two of you met?"

With a quick glance at Vanessa, David smiled. "Yes, right on your door step."

"Oh," Jim said. "The girls wanted to introduce you." Grabbing their jackets, he walked away.

Leaning over, David said low in her ear. "Looks like we're being set up. Third time this year for me. How about you?"

She shook her head. "Second."

A shiver trickled down her spine. Glancing at him, she frowned. "Are we the only singles in the room?"

"From what I can tell, yes."

"Maybe I should leave," she said, feeling uncomfortable. Her New Year's resolution was to find someone this year, but so far between the online dating and her friends, it was like buying a used car from a tote the note lot. Usually, a real dud of a ride.

"No, stay and let's play along to see what kind of game they're up to. Let's have some fun with their scheming. Turn it around on them," he said grinning. "Disco Dave has arrived."

Gazing at the man, she smiled. Disco Dave? That gave her images of bell bottom pants, slicked back hair, and a sleazy smile. This could be interesting. Why not stick around to see what happens? At least, for a little while.

"Just go with me on this," he said, smiling as they walked into the main area. "But remember, it's all an act."

"Vanessa," Brie cried as she ran up to her. "You're here."

"David is here. Have you two met?" Meghan said, coming up to their side. "He's a widower. His wife was a teacher at my school."

Most definitely, this was a set-up. From the corner of her eye, she could see the two of them watching her and David, waiting for a reaction.

"We introduced ourselves at the door. David, I'm so sorry about your wife."

"And Vanessa's husband was killed in Afghanistan three years ago," Brie said with a smile.

Did they realize how horrible they sounded? Sure, they had a common denominator...death.

"Your husband was a soldier?" he asked. "I'm sorry for your loss."

At least he seemed sincere about Kevin's death. The man died fighting for our country and she would not accept his service being tarnished by anyone.

"Thank you," she said, wanting to change the topic. "You really are into Valentine's."

Meghan laughed. "That's when things happened for all of us. I became reacquainted with Max that night. Taylor and Ryan and Kelsey and Cody came together all because the three of us had a little too much wine and did the Cupid dance."

The famous superstition in Cupid, Texas. Dance naked around the fountain at midnight and find your true love because of Thomas Cupid, her husband's great-great-great uncle, who died a lonely man while dancing naked around the fountain.

Max walked up with a tray of drinks and Vanessa took a glass of water. He picked up the story. "Then, because of Cody, Jim, Kyle, and Drew all had to do the Cupid dance at midnight. Only Brie and Stephen Austin did not come together because of our actions that night. They're here to help us celebrate and also met when Brie danced naked around Cupid. So, when are you two planning on sprinting au naturel around the Cupid statue?"

Just taking a sip, Vanessa almost choked on her drink. Sure, she thought of doing the famed dance for love, but something held her back from stripping her clothes off and jogging around the fountain. She'd been to the statue. Had even said farewell to Kevin there, though she sometimes thought she dreamed that night.

"Vanessa, would you like to join me," David said.

Stunned, her brows drew together and he winked suggestively. She had to bite her lip to keep from laughing. The man was acting outrageous.

"That would be an interesting first date. What do you

say? What about Valentine's evening, me and you getting naked in the town square."

While she knew he was joking, everything inside Vanessa cringed at the man's idea. A conservative woman, she wasn't cut out to be part of his game. With a deep breath, she smiled. "I'd be happy to join you there along with the sheriff."

Shaking her head, Brie giggled. "Or Stephen could be waiting for you with handcuffs ready. After all, he arrested his future wife, and I'm certain he would put you in the slammer in a heartbeat."

That's how Vanessa and Brie met—in the Cupid city jail. Not something Vanessa ever planned on repeating. She'd gotten a lucky break and never again would she let her grief overindulge to the point her alcohol intake became drunk driving.

"What about Vanessa?"

Her friend Brie, slipped her arm inside the crook of Vanessa's. "Oh no, this lady is my helper and friend. There will be no going to jail for this woman. Come on, girlfriend, we need to mingle."

The two women hurried away as Brie turned to her. "Sorry, I don't think he's the one for you."

No one seemed to be the right man for her.

"Oh, were you trying to set us up?"

"Not me," Brie said. "Not me. He seemed forward."

"Maybe he's tired of people playing matchmaker."

Brie frowned. "It was that obvious?"

"Oh yes," Vanessa told her friend.

The group walked into the dining room where finger foods were being served buffet style. Brie hurried to join her husband. Vanessa found herself standing next to David in line. As soon as she finished eating and spoke to the other women for a moment, she was out of there.

The man leaned over and whispered, "Really, I'm not a jerk. Let me prove it to you and have dinner with me Valentine's Day."

Turning to stare at him, she gazed into the warmest emerald eyes and a jolt of interest gripped her insides. At first, her reaction was instantly no. Then a little voice said why not? What do you have to lose except spending a lousy night at home remembering all the times with Kevin? Even if it was a complete bust, at least she wouldn't be alone on a couple's holiday.

"Okay, but only if I'm not having dinner with Disco Dave."

"Promise." A mischievous grin spread across his face, creasing his dimples. "Hang on, I'm about to show my dance moves."

Part of her was laughing at the image, but she was also a little nervous. How far was he willing to go to show these people they shouldn't be wasting their time setting him up. And why did she feel like she was going to be the brunt of his bad behavior?

"What are you two whispering about," Meghan asked with a suspicious frown on her face.

"Hey, I'm working my seduction plan, asking her to come back to the house and watch movies," he winked and Vanessa watched as Meghan's eyes widened in shock.

"Only the kind of movies he enjoys are not something I'll watch," Vanessa said trying to play the part.

"Maybe you should concentrate on Vanessa's personality before you try to take her home," Meghan scolded.

With a shrug, David said, "We're two consenting adults. What's to get to know? A woman is a woman."

The first stirrings of anger rode her stomach like a rollercoaster. If this guy acted this way on their date, it could be the shortest date in her history. One thing for certain, David would never be fixed up again by any of her friends.

Everyone stopped and openly stared at the two of them. Brie's facial expression was one of outrage. Any second Vanessa expected her to jump up and do bodily harm to David.

When Vanessa could breathe again, she turned and looked at him. "Sugar," she said softly, "that remark must be the equivalent to the size of your penis. Small minded."

Snickers came from the women while the men in the group looked uncomfortable. Score one for her side.

Grinning at her, his eyes seemed to say touché and she grasped her comment had gotten to him. "Well, darling, I think you should follow me back to my house and let me show you."

"Excuse me," Meghan said loudly. "You just met her."

He shrugged. "We'll see if she's worth a second date."

Vanessa gasped and questioned if she was certain she wanted to go out with this man. How much longer would she stay?

Meghan's face turned red. "Vanessa, I want to apologize to you. In our ignorance, we thought David and you would be good together. The man is not deserving of you."

"Apology accepted," she said with a laugh.

At the moment, Brie couldn't see David's facial expression as he grinned at her. "Setting people up is a crap shoot. Did I get lucky tonight?"

"No, you're hitting a big fat zero," Brie said, walking to her friend.

Biting her lip to keep from laughing out loud, Vanessa actually felt sorry for the girls who had tried to find her someone. Maybe she and David were carrying it a bit too far.

"My other girlfriends don't mind me comparing them to each other. Why should Vanessa be any different? I'm sure she'll be friends with the other girls."

Brie grabbed Vanessa by the arm and pulled her away. "Come on, I'm getting you away from that despicable man. That is uncalled for and I'm so sorry he is here. No one would listen to me and I told them repeatedly this was a bad idea."

His other girlfriends?

Still unsure what she thought about David, Vanessa watched him across the room talking to the men. Looking at her, he winked and a trickle of warmth scattered up her spine. For the first time in years, she had a Valentine date. And it could be a rather interesting night.

CHAPTER 3

On Monday morning, a beautiful bouquet of flowers arrived at the office where Vanessa worked and Brie ran a catering-party planning business.

Brie walked in the door. "Hey, who are those from?"

Remembering how badly David behaved Saturday night, Vanessa smiled. "A friend."

She plopped down in a chair near her desk. "Look, I want to apologize again. None of us could believe his responses to you. Meghan told us his wife was one of the best teachers in the school. Becky always bragged about what a wonderful husband she had and how he took such good care of her while she was sick. At the funeral there was no question he was devastated. Maybe he changed after her death. Grief affects people differently."

This morning Vanessa heard from each one of her

friends as they apologized and said they had no idea David could be such a jerk. In some ways, she almost felt like she should be honest and confide in them that they had both been acting.

Their friends had their wellbeing in mind, but she was tired of them trying to set her up with a man. Let her find her own significant other. Though, right now, that person must have gotten lost on his way to Cupid.

"Forget it ever happened. Maybe next time don't try to hook me up. This is the third time and everyone's attempts have not worked out very well."

"You're right," she said smiling. "The rest of us are happy and we want the same for you."

"Yes, I want that too, but so far no one I would consider as husband material has appeared on the horizon. Time for us all to take a deep breath, step back, and let fate be the one who decides when I'll get my second chance at love."

Though Kevin had been gone for three years, it felt like only yesterday. Vanessa wanted to find love, but dating was different than in college and she was picky about who would take his place.

Brie sighed heavily. "Fate needs to get off her ass and move a little faster. The plan is for our kids to grow up together and you're getting behind in that department."

With complete surprise, Vanessa stopped and gazed at Brie. "Really? You're pregnant?"

"Per the plus sign on the stick, we're a go. Baby Austin should be arriving in early November."

Happiness for her friend filled Vanessa, but inside her gut twisted with jealousy. Would she ever be that happy again?

Brie and Stephen's wedding had barely been six months ago, but they wanted to start on their family right away. Neither of them were getting any younger, and Stephen, who had recently been reunited with his mother, wanted his children to know their grandmother.

Vanessa ran around the desk and grabbed her friend, giving her a hug. "Oh my, I'm so happy for you. How excited is Stephen?"

"He doesn't know. I'm waiting to tell him at dinner on Valentine's Day."

What a joyful occasion for the two of them and for just a small moment, Vanessa wanted to cry. Brie had what she wanted. A happy life with a man who adored her and the two of them were now creating their own family. The couple had gone through a lot to find love and she would do the same for the right man.

"What a surprise. He's going to be so thrilled."

That also meant she would need to tell David they couldn't go to the only restaurant in Cupid. Then again, they both knew Taylor's family diner would be packed with people from town as she and Ryan had the only place in town to eat. They always made Valentine's dinner a big event.

"This will be our first Valentine's Day as a married couple. What I have planned is super romantic," Brie said with a smile. "Everything is ready. He's going to be so surprised."

Again, the green-eyed monster bit Vanessa hard, but that didn't mean she was sour for her friend. She just wished it was her.

At least this year she wouldn't be alone, but rather with David. Though that thought sent a cringe shivering through her, leaving her a little unsettled. She had no idea who to expect. The friendly man she met on the porch or Disco Dave who made her think twice about their date.

CHAPTER 4

*D*avid sat in the teacher's lounge grading papers from his logistics class. When the door opened, he looked up.

"Did you have too much to drink the other night?" Max asked as he stared at him. "In the years I've known you, you've never behaved like that."

David shrugged, not wanting to let his friend be privy to exactly what happened. "Not a drop of alcohol."

"What was that nonsense about your other girl-friends? What were you talking about? You're the biggest loner I know."

How did he respond without telling the truth, and while he would eventually confess, right now he wanted to keep his secrets until he went on a date with Vanessa. The woman had been amazing to put up with his shenanigans. That didn't mean much as far as dating, but she was attractive and fun, and he did indeed want to check her out a little further.

"I resemble that statement. Dating is not the same. A couple times, I went out with some of the ladies from church and then only the losers my friends have insisted I try."

"After Saturday night, I think we all know who the loser is," Max said, shaking his head.

David grinned. The act should at least slow his friends from getting more ideas.

Intent on stopping his friends from setting him up again, at the party he acted like the kind of man he hated. The slimy, sleazy type of loser who dated more than one woman at a time and only wanted one thing from them. That conjured an image he would never be like and that's who he'd become, Disco Dave.

"Did you know I spent two hours talking Meghan out of going after you. She wanted me to turn you into the school board for your inappropriate behavior."

"For what? Hitting on her friend?"

"No, for being a lousy jerk. Finally, she settled with a promise that I would never leave you with any of our children since she thinks you're into pornography."

He grinned. No problem there. Not even a risqué movie in his house. Not unless you considered his wife's romance DVD collection as lewd.

"From the looks she was sending me, I knew she was

upset. As a single man, you have to understand it's a new set-up weekly." He sighed. "It gets old."

From now on, this was his response to any match-making attempts by his friends. Disco Dave would soon stop everyone from trying to find him a woman.

"The women wanted to castrate you. Good thing you left. It could have gotten ugly," Max said. "Shame you brought your nasty side to show Vanessa. After being around her a couple times, I know she's a lovely woman."

According to his friends, they were all love-ly women. Every time he was set up, they promised him this was the woman for him. Becky had been his girl and she was dead. A vicious disease, breast cancer, took her from him way too soon.

After several bad blind dates, he was ready to give up on dating.

"Well, you don't have to worry about them trying to find you a woman any longer. No worries there, my friend."

Perfect, he didn't want them interfering, even though they had good intentions. Yes, he longed to meet another woman, but was it wrong to want to do it on his terms? When the right girl came along he would know. For now, he kept looking.

Vanessa had been a sport about how he acted last night. Most women would have thrown him under the bus, then run over him more than once for his bad acting. This morning he sent her bouquet of daisies and chrysanthemums as an apology and asked if on their date they might start fresh.

"So did you at least get her number?" Max asked.

"Not exactly," he lied, not wanting his friend to know the truth. "She wasn't speaking to me, when she left."

Max shook his head. "Serves you right."

If their night out was anything like his past experiences with women, it would be one and done. Usually it was one long night at a restaurant with a lady he would soon realize he shared nothing in common with. If the night was terribly boring, he would make an excuse to end the date early and dive into a book, with the television turned off and all the reminders this was the night of love blocked.

More like the loneliest night of the year.

CHAPTER 5

*V*alentine's Day finally arrived and Vanessa just wanted the night to end. Could this be yet another bad date?

Nervous, she dressed in a pair of elegant silk pants and a top that shimmered in the light. The heels she chose she could yank off and run if needed or use as a weapon. Disco Dave better be back in the closet where he belonged.

While David seemed like a gentleman, his performance the other night left her cautious. She feared who she would have dinner with and Disco Dave was a definite no go. She'd be out the door and back home before her appetite was quenched.

They agreed he would cook for her at his house tonight and that only added to her already thinly-stretched nerves. Pulling into his driveway, she stared at the bungalow sitting in a decent neighborhood. A lonely dog barked somewhere in the distance and she tried to calm her agitated stomach. After getting out of the car, she walked up to the house and pressed the bell.

The door opened and he stood there.

"Hi," he said, giving her a brief hug as she walked in. Across the room, a fireplace radiated warmth in the chilly Texas evening.

The house was nothing like she expected. After their first meeting, she thought Disco Dave would live in the typical bachelor pad—beer cans, pizza boxes, and dirty underwear lying around. But instead, his home was warm and inviting.

Licking her lips, she tried to calm her shaking hands. If she felt uncomfortable, all she had to do was make an excuse and leave.

"Hi," she said as he helped her with her coat. "Happy Valentine's Day."

"Happy Valentine's Day to you as well," he said.

"Thank you for the flowers. That was very thoughtful," she said. The last bouquet she received had been roses from Kevin and it was nice to replace that memory with a new one. Their scent and blooms had improved her day.

A smile crossed his face. "After my behavior the other night, it seemed the least I could do," he said, staring at her. "Disco Dave had a short life and you'll soon see I'm really not that guy."

What could she say except that if Disco made an appearance, he would watch her walk out the door. The end. Finale.

"I think I met him online. Let me just say he's a lousy date and not worthy of my time."

A chuckle came from David.

Placing his hand on her elbow, David led her into the kitchen. "The weather is warm enough, so I'm grilling steaks. I hope you're not vegan. Would you like a glass of wine?"

"I like meat," she said following him. Glancing around, she adored the way the kitchen was bedecked with an Italian flair. Bottles sat on an upper shelf with artificial ivy entwined amongst them, a bowl of wine corks sat on the counter.

"Beautiful kitchen," she said.

The thought crossed her mind that his wife must have done the decorating, and yet in her own situation, she had redecorated everything after Kevin's death by up and selling their home.

"Thanks." Pausing, he stopped and stared at her. "Oh my, you're the first woman who has been here since my wife died. Most of the time, I would just meet women at the diner."

"Well, I feel honored that I'm the first," she said.

"Yeah, well don't get too excited. My dating score-card is not doing real well," he said. "I'm striking out with zero home runs."

That certainly made her stop and think. Why was he striking out so much?

"How many second dates have you had," she asked gently.

Laughing, he said, "Zero."

"Me too. One date is enough for me to know it doesn't feel right."

He glanced at her and smiled. "Seems we have something in common. Are we lousy partners or just picky."

"Picky," she immediately replied.

"Same."

As he stirred a pot, she watched. "What are you fixing?"

"Sorry, my favorite. Macaroni and cheese. A baked potato would have been better for us."

"Mac and cheese is one of my favorites as well. Perfect."

"That's two things in common," he said.

"At least one of them is a good thing," she replied.

Smiling, he glanced out the door.

"Let me help you," she said, realizing he wanted to check on the grill. "I'll stir while you take care of the steaks."

"Give me a moment, I'll be right back," he said, stepping out the door. In less than a minute, he returned. "They're almost done."

"So the girls called me on Monday and apologized for trying to bring us together."

"Max chewed me out and told me that Meghan wanted to turn me into the school board for my inappropriate behavior."

"The school board? Really?" she said. She knew Meghan was a very smart stickler for the rules, but what did she think she was going to turn David in for? Being a sleaze bag?

"Meghan is the best, but she does believe in playing by the rules. My comments were way out of line according to her," David said, standing in the kitchen watching her stir.

"Brie promised me she would never try to matchmake me with anyone again and she would stop anyone who tried."

Walking up beside her, he picked up the pan and drained the noodles. Then she put in the slices of real cheddar and began to stir, letting the cheese slowly melt.

"That's nice."

"Do you think we're off the hook with them?" she asked, wondering if it was true.

"No, but my acting bought us a reprieve for a little while. Three years have passed since Becky's death. I'll find someone at the right time on my own."

They both lost their partners around the same time.

While it seemed recently, she knew she was over his death and ready to move forward with the right man.

Vanessa's eyes widened. "Kevin died three years ago. And you're right, eventually, I'll remarry or so I hope. For a while, I tried online dating, but it turned into a total waste of time. The site was into hookups. Not for me."

After the third unsuccessful date, she'd known she was done. Each time, it seemed the man expected to take her back to his place or her place and they were going to have sex. What was wrong with getting to know someone before you saw them naked?

"You're a lot braver than me. Scrolling through the website, I checked out the rules and decided not now, maybe later. Besides my friends' set-ups, I dated a couple women from the church we attended. Not a good thing because everyone assumes you're going to marry. No, just no."

The table was already set with salad bowls, linen napkins, their goblets, and glasses of water. Salad dressing and even a few steak sauces were sitting out. The man knew how to set a table.

"The food is ready. Let me bring in the steaks," he said.

As he took the meat off the grill, she gazed around at the living room of the house. Bookshelves lined one wall, a large television hung opposite, with a fireplace in the center. The house appeared well decorated and she thought he'd done a great job of pulling it all together to make it feel like a home.

Walking in, he placed the dish on the table and hurried to the stove and put the macaroni and cheese in a bowl.

"Let's eat," he said, pulling out her chair.

Like a gentleman, he seated her, and a moment later, joined her, sitting across the table. He lifted his goblet. "Since this is our first date and a day dedicated to love, I have a toast." She raised her glass. "To each of us finding a second chance at love."

They clinked their glasses together and took a sip of wine.

"How long were you married before your wife became ill," she asked as she took a bite of steak.

"We were married five years when she received her diagnosis of cancer. The type of breast cancer was one of the more aggressive forms and no matter what they did, they couldn't cure her. Becky endured so much going through surgery, chemo, and radiation." With a heartfelt sigh, he continued. "Watching someone you love suffer, knowing there's nothing you can do to help them, is hard."

A shared sense of pain gripped her heart and she ached for him. "No children?"

"No, we never conceived, though she wanted a baby so badly," he said, staring at her. "But we had each other."

This conversation couldn't get more morbid, she

thought. If he asked about Kevin, it would only go downhill further and she had to somehow bring back the joy of the evening.

"Tell me something that you and your wife did together that you miss," she said, hoping that would tell her more about him.

"Camping. We loved to get away, build a fire, snuggle and just sit and talk. Years have passed since my sleeping bag has been rolled out."

Silence permeated the table, but it wasn't uncomfortable, more like a warm sigh filled with happy memories of people they once loved.

"Your husband was killed in Afghanistan?" he asked.

"Yes, his Humvee ran over an explosive device, killing him instantly," she said, remembering the day the car pulled up in front of her home and the military personnel stepped out. The memory of her heart slamming into her throat while a cry ripped from her chest. No words were needed as the two soldiers in their dress uniform approached. Their somber expressions said the words she never wanted to hear. "Kevin went off to war and I never saw him again."

"That's tough," he said.

Not seeing him again wasn't exactly true, but she didn't tell anyone about their meeting at the fountain. The logical side of her brain told her she was hallucinating with grief while her heart said it was true—Kevin said goodbye. Either way, that moment was way too personal to share with anyone. Time to change the subject and speak about something other than death.

"You're a teacher?" she asked.

"A coach," he said. "Varsity baseball, and I teach one class on logistics."

Well, he couldn't be all bad if he was around children all day. There were background checks for working in schools. Still, she felt a little wary of him, but not as much. "Tell me why you are a teacher."

"Since I was a kid, I've played ball. In college, I was on varsity and anticipated playing for a professional team, but senior year, I blew out my knee blocking second base. The doctor said I was done, and I said, oh hell no, I'm not finished with this game. My dreams of a big career were gone, but I could still coach and teach. Baseball is pretty much my life. In the summer, I work with the little league and during the school year, I'm coaching high school."

As he talked about the game, his face brightened and he became animated telling her he enjoyed what he did. So far, this David seemed like a nice man with a comfortable life. But the verdict was still out.

"From the way you talk, I can tell you enjoy what you do."

"Sure, I would love to play professional ball, but some things were never meant to be. Now, I enjoy watching the kids grow and learn," he said as they finished eating. "Come on, let's watch the flames in the fireplace and talk. Tell me the one thing you miss doing with your husband."

They grabbed their glasses as they walked from the table. Sitting on the sofa, he pulled a blanket off the back and wrapped it around their legs. "This will keep us nice and toasty."

It was the first time she could remember sitting beside a man, their shoulders touching, gazing at the fire as they sipped their Chardonnay and savored each other's company. So far, this night had been more fun than she expected, but she still felt a little uncertain as to how the evening would end.

"There are so many things I miss about Kevin, but mainly, the way he would wrap his arms around me at night. In the darkness, we always cuddled until sleep overcame us. Later, we would separate, but even then, I would wake to hear him breathing and be comforted he was beside me and my world was safe."

Since his death, her bed had been cold and lonely, and at night, she still missed the feel of his arms around her.

With a nod, David said, "We both have good recollections of marriage. This discussion is so much better than listening to someone tell me how mean their ex was to them and all the baggage they carried."

Oh yes, she'd dated a man who she feared would locate his wife and do her bodily harm. He hated her so much that Vanessa would never step into her place.

After that, she put another box on her list of do's and don'ts on the dating website. No one recently separated or divorced. Was it wrong to want what she had with Kevin?

"Yes, but we also have baggage. Our wonderful memories help us remember what we're missing. And also remind us that whoever and whenever we marry the next time, we want someone to create those special remembrances with again. That could be why I'm being so picky this time. When you had an exceptional marriage, your expectations are the same the second time around."

While she would never date or marry a soldier again, Kevin had been a strong influence, a great man who only occasionally made her angry. Only when his military background took over and he became too controlling. Then she would have to make certain he knew there were two in this marriage who made their decisions together.

David's arm came around her shoulder and he squeezed her to him. "Nicely put as I never thought of it that way, but I know what I want and expect. Once you've had a great love, it's harder to find another one."

"Great loves don't just fall into your lap. Could that be the reason we're both tired of people trying to fix us up?"

Simultaneously they started laughing. "Last night was kind of fun," he said. "But paybacks..."

"You should have been an actor. You played the part well," she said smiling.

"Thanks, I think," he said.

"They'll all get over it, once they know the truth. For now, I don't want to tell them anything different," Vanessa said, thinking that she was enjoying tonight, but if everyone learned their plan, they would start pressuring them.

With a pause, his eyes narrowed and he thought for a moment. "That could mean one of two things. Either you think I'm the jerk you met that night, or you want to give us a chance without everyone making a big deal."

"You got it," she said. "Right now, I'm leaning toward door number two. Keeping everything on the down low. You haven't told me what you think about our date."

Wondering what he was thinking, she looked at him shyly.

Pulling her in tighter, he leaned into her, his lips covered hers, his tongue gently pushing into her mouth. He tasted of fruity wine and happiness and commitment and all the things absent in her life. He tasted like a man she could possibly consider seeing again.

Leaning back, she licked her lips, missing him already. "That was nice."

"Does that answer your question?" he asked. "Tonight has been the most promising date in years. Would you go out with me on Saturday? What if we drive to

Granbury and explore the shops? Have dinner and then return."

"What time will you pick me up?"

With a smile, his mouth covered hers once more. This Valentine's Day was the best she'd experienced in a long time.

CHAPTER 6

On Saturday, Vanessa dressed warmly in her yoga pants and boots, a sweater scarf wrapped around her neck. The Valentine's date felt natural. Like she'd spent the evening with an old friend. They'd sat in front of the fire, sipping wine, talking, getting to know one another and laughing.

David was smart, funny, and for the first time since Kevin, she might have found someone to date. If it went further great, but right now, she just longed to have fun. To spend time learning about David. To laugh and smile and forget about the bad times.

The bell rang and she pulled open the door. "Hi."

"Hi," he said, coming in and kissing her full on the mouth. A tingle of awareness spiraled through her as he pushed her in the house. Finally, she broke free of his lips. "Aren't we going to Granbury?"

"Yes, but first I wanted to see your home. After all, you saw mine," he said.

"Oh," she replied with a smile.

"Love the fact you live on the river."

"Yes, I bought this house not long after Kevin died. We always wanted to live here, so I decided, I would."

The money she received after his death she used to purchase this home. While she loved living here, it was lonely being out of town away from everything, and she had considered putting it on the market. But that decision was for another day.

"Do you have much wildlife around here?" he asked.

"Deer, skunks, and the occasional beaver. Oh, and in the summer, drunks."

"Yes, I'm sure plenty of parties float down the river when the weather is warm," he said with a laugh.

"When the Brazos is high enough," she said.

"Come on, let's go. Your house is nice, but we have a bit of a drive and things to do."

A tremor of nerves scurried up her spine. It was one thing to go to a man's house with her own car, but now she was trusting him to drive her an hour away and spend the day with him. Trust didn't come overnight and with each date, she would learn more and more about him.

"What kind of things?" she asked.

"Oh no, you'll just have to wait and see," he said,

taking her hand and pulling her out the door. After locking up behind her, they walked to his car. The door being opened for her, she climbed into a red Corvette. "Wow, I'm impressed."

"You bought a house after your husband passed. I bought a sports car."

As he slid into the driver's seat, she said, "Crazy what grief can do to you."

"Say that again," he said as he put the car in gear and pulled onto the road in front of her home. "What other kooky things did you do?"

Sinking back into the seat, she watched as he handled the car expertly and realized she liked his confidence.

"One night, I wrote every congressman and told them this war was not worth losing my husband over. Then I divided his things with his mother and she took some and I took a few. Two months after his death, I couldn't sleep. In the middle of the night, I got up, packed everything in our house and the next day called a moving truck. And here I am."

With a quick glance at her, he reached over and squeezed her leg right above her knee and left his hand there.

"What about you? What kind of crazy things did you do?"

"After everyone left, I buried myself in a whiskey bottle for a week, until Max came over and straightened me out. Told me to get my ass back to work. This was not what Becky would have wanted. And he was right."

Him staring at her, she knew he was looking for how his admission affected her. The idea of drinking had crossed her mind, but alcohol left her feeling lousy and only made her sadder. She had learned that the hard way when she'd been arrested for a DUI. It was how she met Brie who rescued her and kept her record clean.

"Six months later, when I thought I was doing better, I started hanging out at Valentino's bar - dancing. Met a weird woman who showed me I wasn't ready to date. Did you have someone like that?"

"No, I didn't even start dating again until Kevin had been gone over eighteen months," she said thinking of how lonely she'd been, but knew the time wasn't right. "What did you do after that?"

"Went back to church and dated several women I knew and quickly made the decision against seeing women who knew us as a couple. Went on a few blind dates and decided I was finished with women forever. No more. I'm done and then you showed up on the doorstep of Jim and Shadow's home."

This was the first time Vanessa had been on a second date. All her dating experiences were one and done. No more. "Blind dates are the worst."

"Yes," he agreed. "Yet our friends tried to set up the two of us and here we are on officially our second date, but the third time to hang out."

She smiled and glanced at him. "Wouldn't they be surprised to see us? That first time was a little rough," she said. "Sure, we talked about tricking them, but I began to doubt if the man introduced to me on the porch was the same one that attended the party."

"Now you know differently," he said.

So far, she believed it had all been a big act. She hoped so because David had lasted longer than any man before him. While they still had a long way to go, she felt comfortable with him and enjoyed his company.

"Yes," she finally said.

"So here is my grand plan for today's date. The square is a neat place to do shopping and exploring. Afterwards, dinner on the lake at this really nice restaurant where we could watch the sun go down. Unless there's something specific you want to do."

Vanessa gazed at the man with dark brown hair and eyes that twinkled with an iridescent green. Her mind wanted to compare him to Kevin and she shut it down. This time belonged to David and the present, not the past. And she liked his looks. She liked them a lot, and so far she enjoyed his mind.

"Sounds like a lovely day. The sky is a brilliant blue and it's supposed to be in the sixties. What could possibly go wrong?"

"Don't say that," he scolded. "You'll jinx us."

"You're superstitious? I bet you believe in the Cupid..." she stopped. The vision that night of a man fixated on the statue after she had spoken to Kevin struck her. Mouth open, she turned to him. "Now, I remember you. Where I saw you."

"What?" he said, unable to take his eyes off the road as they were in heavy traffic.

"It was Christmas over a year ago. The park was empty and dark. As I walked away from the God of Love, you were staring up at that carved chunk of rock and you asked me if I believed in the town superstition."

An eerie shiver went through her and she thought of the Cupid superstition. Could it work even with clothes on? But neither had ran around the statue or even chanted the verse. Yet here they were together. But she also had an odd tie to the man who created the superstition.

David licked his lips and glanced at her. "Yes, I was there. That's why you looked so familiar the other night. We spoke about the statue."

"Yes, you asked me if I was going to do the dance and I said no," she whispered. "Did you run around the statue naked that night?"

Shaking his head, he gave her a look before turning his attention back to the highway. "Oh no. After running into you, I walked the path past the boy in the diaper and realized I could never do that naked. So, I went home. That Christmas was hard."

"Yes," she said quietly as they entered the small town of Granbury.

David had been the first man she'd seen after saying goodbye to Kevin. Could he be the one meant for her? Was this why neither of them had found someone to love, because they were meant to be together?

It all seemed impossible.

They drove around the courthouse until he found a parking spot. Swirling to face her in the seat, he took her hand. "Something that night so long ago told me you were special. This is only our second official date, but it feels easy and natural between us."

She smiled because that described her feelings as well.

Reaching over, she pulled his lips to hers and kissed him softly. "As long as bad David doesn't return, there might be something here worth checking out."

Grinning, he jumped out of the car and raced around to her side and opened the door for her. "Come on, let's enjoy this beautiful day. We deserve this."

CHAPTER 7

A month later, the weather had started warming, but the breeze held a chill and they still had not told their friends they were dating. Brie kept looking at Vanessa strangely and even told her she seemed happier. And she was.

David and she grew closer every day, and he made her smile and enjoy life once again. Once a week, she cooked him dinner and he did the same for her. They laughed and joked, and each day, their kisses became more passionate.

Nothing sexual had happened yet and she felt certain he was waiting on her, but anxiety had her stomach in knots. The only man she ever slept with had been Kevin and their first time together happened on their wedding night.

Time rushed at her, leaving her restless and nervous

and unable to sleep for dreaming of David. She wasn't against sleeping with the man, but she waited, needing to know if this growing romance was real. Call her old fashioned, but she needed to be certain she loved him. Then she would consider having sex with him, but not until. Not until they had a commitment to each other.

A knock on the door sounded and she hurried to let him in. "Let's go."

"Where are we off to this time?" she asked as his lips found hers and he kissed her, pulling her against him.

"Hmmm, keep kissing me like that and we may stay here and make out on the couch," he said, biting her earlobe gently.

A shiver ran through her that ended in her center with her breathing harsh. One thing about David, there was no lack of chemistry between them. Whenever he touched her, her body heated from the inside out with a need that reminded her of pleasure she had forgotten.

"Let's go," she whispered huskily.

"To be continued," he said, grabbing her by the hand and helping her out the door.

Running down her steps, they raced to his car. "You didn't answer my question."

"Nope, I didn't. It's Friday night. I feel the need for gazing at the stars and resting from a disturbing week," he said.

"Kicking out your top players is stressful?"

"Absolutely," he said. "Everyone on the team is affected."

This week he'd been forced to expel two kids he thought highly of, but who screwed up badly. For days, she witnessed him trying to decide what to do and finally reaching the conclusion, they deserved their punishment.

Once they were on the road, she glanced in the back. "A sleeping bag?"

"To keep us warm," he said. "I'm taking you to the woods to have my way with you."

She hoped he was teasing. Every day, her feelings grew stronger for him, but she wasn't ready for that next step just yet. Soon, but not yet.

"Just kidding," he said, glancing at her worriedly. "Though the idea is tempting."

Reaching over, she laid her hand on his knee. "For a moment, you had me worried that Disco Dave had resurfaced. Professionals say it takes at least six months to really get to know someone."

"My parents married three months after they met," he said. "No, they didn't know each other well, but they were together for over fifty years."

Nodding, she thought about her own family situation and shuddered. "Mine divorced when I was five."

Turning to look at her, he said, "You never told me that."

"Unlike your parents, they dated for two years before

they said I do. Maybe they should have just lived together."

It was true. Her family had fallen apart not long after her younger brother, Jason, was born. Now her mother and father were gone, and Jason was off doing his own tour of duty. Her brother introduced her to Kevin.

"That explains a lot about your wariness and your need to learn as much about me as possible," he said. "Frankly, it shows me how smart you are."

"Thank you," she said.

"But that doesn't mean I'm not going to push your boundaries," he said smiling. "We've been dating a month. Time for us to start thinking about what happens next."

Shaking her head in disagreement, she stared as he turned onto the lake road. "Not yet," she said softly, then abruptly changed the subject. "Where are we going?"

"We're going to build a bonfire and make s'mores and drink hot chocolate and cuddle around the fire."

Though many women would find it boring, she couldn't think of a better way to spend the evening. Besides, the man enjoyed the outdoors, and relaxing around a fire was the perfect stress reliever for him. "Tell me, what happened to the boys?"

A deep sigh escaped him. "Three days expulsion, which will drop their grades and they'll miss the first two weeks of baseball. My season could be ruined."

His dreams of winning a state championship

sounded to be on hold as long as these boys were suspended and missing games. After seeing how hard he worked with his team, she wanted him to win. To earn the recognition he deserved.

An ache for him centered in her chest. "As much as it hurts, you did the right thing."

"Hope so," he said. "Now, I'd just like to win without them. We'll see what happens."

One of the first things she'd learned about David was that he was competitive, not in a mean sense, but rather with his sports. Yes, he wanted his kids to learn, but he also liked success. And she was learning to like baseball.

The car came to a stop at a campsite not far from the water. "Come on," he said. "Let's get a nice blaze going and then we'll watch the moon rise over the lake."

"Nice," she said, knowing tonight would be both wonderful and difficult. Wonderful because she would be spending time with David experiencing the emotions and desires he created, but difficult, because she knew she couldn't sleep with him yet. Suddenly she wondered if she would ever be ready to have a sexual relationship with another man.

CHAPTER 8

*D*avid finished building the fire and then sank down on the ground behind Vanessa, wrapping his arms around her and pulling the sleeping bag around the two of them. The cold night air caressed their cheeks, but inside they were snuggly warm. With her back against his chest, a sense of peace overcame him.

This woman surprised him. After this long, he hadn't expected to find another chance at happiness, but every day, he could feel himself falling more and more for this fun-loving woman.

At this time in his life, he was ready to find a woman to enjoy being with, have a couple kids, and share the heartaches that came with existing. The ups and downs of everyday living while leaning on each other. Vanessa had all the qualities he liked in a partner and he wondered about the two of them together.

"Why didn't you have children with Kevin?" he asked, needing to know if she wanted a family.

"One last tour of duty and then we would begin our family, he promised. The plan was for him to stay in the military, but be stateside - and not return to Afghanistan. Kevin wanted to be there and watch our children grow. How could I deny him that opportunity? So I agreed to one more stint. Only he never came home."

David sensed her disappointment. As a woman, she must have wanted to have his child in case anything happened to him and then when it did, she had to have felt some anger. "So, you want children."

"With the right man, of course. Now, so many of my friends either have children or they're expecting. That big birthday is racing toward me, and my time is running out. Last year, I considered doing the turkey baster procedure and having a child on my own."

What in the world was she talking about? "The turkey baster procedure?"

"A sperm donor. It all seemed so cold that I promised myself one more year before I took that final step. Why did you and Becky wait so long before you tried?"

Guilt ate at him as he remembered how she had pushed for them to start their family. At the time, he wanted their student loans paid off before they had kids. Those two years of waiting had cost her the opportunity of having a child. Then when they tried, Becky learned she had breast cancer.

"It was my fault we waited. Maybe if we went ahead, she would have gotten the chance to hold a baby in her arms, but maybe not. I don't know. If there is a next time, I'm not waiting. Nothing is going to get in the way of a family this time," he said softly, burying his nose in her hair and breathing in her scent. "In fact, I'm willing and ready to begin right now if you are?"

The words were said in such a way, he hoped it sounded like he was teasing, but he was serious. While the idea that the first time should be special was something he believed in, right here under the stars couldn't be any better.

She turned and stared at him. "Not yet. Our dating has been fun. I'm having a great time with you, but I'm not rushing into anything. Besides, we haven't even told our friends we're dating."

Early on, they decided to keep things quiet between them so as not to put demands on the relationship or themselves. "You're right," he said, nuzzling her neck. "Tell me when you're ready, and we will tell them together. We'll move at your speed, so let me know when to take the next step."

Somehow, he got the feeling Vanessa didn't sleep

around. Hell, who was he kidding, one-night stands and booty calls didn't fit his personality either. When you never had a second date, you didn't find yourself in the bedroom.

Smiling, she turned and pulled him to the ground, her lips covering his as he let her take the lead. She moved her mouth over his, demanding, her tongue sliding between his lips, he so wanted to claim her as his own, but knew patience was required.

As she lay on top of him, her breasts smashed against his chest, her womanly center placed over his manhood, it was all he could do to keep from rolling her onto her back and taking what he wanted. Pressure rose inside him, threatening his control, until she released his mouth and opened her eyes. He stared into sapphire eyes that left him quivering with need.

"That should prove to you I'm enjoying spending time with you. There's a possibility of this turning into something serious. Please, I'm not ready to wake up naked in your bed. Not yet."

Images of the two of them together, her flesh against his filled his head and his dreams had him clutching her to him. More and more, he felt certain about Vanessa. For the first time in years, he was happy and optimistic about the future.

With a groan he gasped, "Why did you mention the word naked? My mind immediately started picturing the two of us, and well, let's just say we were having a really good time."

Rising from him, she laughed. "Keep it PG, please."

"Not on your life," he said growling. "To stay out of trouble, we should make some s'mores and cleanse my mind of our first night together."

CHAPTER 9

$\mathcal{A}$fter their night sitting around a campfire, Vanessa decided they needed to be more public. It was hard to have a hot and heavy make out session in a bar, especially with other people around. Years had passed, since she'd been out boot scooting.

The next Saturday night, they went to Valentino's Bar, the only place in Cupid where you could dance and listen to country and western music. Gazing around the joint at the people there, she took pleasure in figuring out who was married and who was single. The single women gathered with their friends, drinking and laughing and checking out the men.

The available men reclined against the railing, trying to appear cool while checking out the tables full of women. The married couples sat with friends, talking and occasionally getting on the floor. David and Vanessa sat at their own little table right next to each other's shoulders, rubbing together as they talked and teased one another.

Just a look from David sent a tingle of awareness skittering along her spine, straight to her groin creating a heat long forgotten. A sensual desire that begged to be fulfilled and she pondered why she was waiting.

Was it fear or some other reason she was putting off sleeping with the man? David was the only person other than Kevin she had considered having sex with, and yet she was dragging her feet.

Last time she recalled, she really enjoyed sex. Making love had been wonderful and fulfilling and brought the man she loved close. There had been a commitment between them, a promise of forever, but with David, she didn't have that assurance.

"Come on," he said. "Let's dance."

"Okay," she said and stood from her chair. Taking her by the hand, the two walked onto the sawdust-covered concrete floor and she slid into his arms like that was where she belonged.

This felt so right, so good, and she didn't want the music to end. The feel of his arms around her filled her with longing. His scent surrounded her, his body sliding against her own as they danced. For a moment, she laid her head on his shoulder and sighed.

"That was a deep sigh," he said.

"Yes, this is so nice," she replied. "Dancing with you is..."

"Dancing with you, makes it hard to face my bed alone," he whispered.

"Yes," she groaned.

Opening her eyes, movement at the door drew her attention. There in the entrance way stood Kelsey and Cody along with Meghan and Max. She tensed and he leaned back. "What's wrong?"

"Oh no, our friends just walked in the door."

With a jerk, he whirled around and saw them standing there. The couples were looking in the opposite direction. No one had spotted them yet.

"Let's go," she said.

"Oh come on," he said, his voice sounding irritated. "Let's go talk to them and say hello."

Panic overwhelmed her, gripping her chest. "No, I'm not ready to be grilled about our relationship. Don't let them ruin what we have. I'll meet you out in the parking lot."

Releasing him, she walked over to the table, grabbed her coat and slipped out the exit door before anyone saw her, leaving David behind.

A few minutes later, David met her at the car. In the dark, she could see his expression was hard as stone, his eyes were flashing with indignation and his body looked stiff. From his body language, she could tell he was not happy.

When he didn't open her door, she got the message, he was mad. Part of her understood why he felt that way, but she refused to be rushed by anyone.

Starting his Corvette, they drove away in silence, not speaking the entire drive. Coming to a stop at her house, he escorted her to the door and when she unlocked the entry, she turned to him. "Come in and let's talk. We're having our first argument."

Walking inside, he turned to her, his eyes flashing with hurt. "Are you ashamed to be seen with me?"

"Of course not," she said. "How could you say that when I was just in a bar with you."

Was she being selfish wanting to keep their dating a secret. When their friends learned the truth, there would be so many questions and then the pressure would mount for them to marry. Right now, she liked what they had.

"Then why are you so insistent that we keep our dating a secret? Believe me, I'm ready to yell it to everyone and you act like you're embarrassed of me. Are you certain you're ready for a relationship, because I keep sensing uncertainty from you."

That was not what she wanted to hear. The uncertainty he was sensing was her reluctance to sleep with him, though she wanted to.

Grabbing his hand, she led him to the couch and sat next to him.

"David, you are the first man to get past my

walls. I'm sorry, I'm taking things so slow, but I need to know we're meant for each other before I let other people see us together. You are a fine man and I'm so happy we're dating. Please, give me a little more time. Once I'm certain about us, then we can have a coming out party."

He laughed. "That's a thought."

Sighing, he picked up her hand and glanced into her eyes. "Can I ask you a very personal question?"

With a shrug, she gazed at him wondering what he was going to ask. "Of course."

Licking his lips, he squeezed her hand. "Believe me when I say I'm not judging, but rather trying to understand you. Becky and I had sex five months after we met. By that time, I planned on asking her to marry me. We were sure about our love. How soon did you and Kevin?"

This was the question she dreaded answering, and yet she didn't know why. Who she slept with was her choice and only her decision to make. "We waited until our wedding night, and yes, he was my first."

Nodding, he said, "That makes things clearer for me. Now, I understand."

Fear filled her and she had to make certain he understood, because she didn't want to lose him, and yet in a way, it was a test for them both.

"It's not that I don't want to have sex with you, I do. But I'm not a woman who jumps in and out of bed with just anyone. While I don't require a ceremony and a ring, I do need to make certain I love you."

Pulling her to him, he hugged her and kissed the top of her head.

"I'm falling in love with you. Every day more and more, I miss you. You're the first person I think of in the morning and the last thought before I close my eyes. Don't panic. I'm not ready to get down on bended knee, but I am ready for the two of us to be a couple in front of the world and defend our relationship from anyone who would try to end it. Does that make sense?"

Laying her head against his chest, she felt comforted in knowing he was falling for her. Happiness swelled inside her like a warm balloon filling her chest.

"Yes," she whispered. "And just like you, I'm falling for you, but I'm scared. What if something happens to you? What if I lose you?"

Gripping her face with his hands, he stared in her eyes. "If I can help it, I'm not going anywhere. For the first time in a long time, I'm happy."

"Me too," she said as his lips crushed hers beneath his own, his mouth proving to her how much he cared and how much he wanted her. Now, more than ever, she knew it was only a matter of time.

CHAPTER 10

*T*he next day at lunch in Taylor's diner, Brie sat across from Vanessa staring at her. "You seem down today."

"No, just got something on my mind. How are you feeling? I noticed you ate your lunch."

The woman smiled. "Lunch is good, but breakfast is a no go. Until eleven o'clock, and then it's like there's a switch turned on and I can eat. Until then, don't even talk to me about food unless you want me throwing up on you."

Vanessa smiled and watched Taylor going around to different tables filling people's ice tea glasses, smiling, and talking.

"There must be a man in your life, because you've been acting pretty strange lately," Brie said.

With a jerk, Vanessa turned her attention back to Brie.

"Oh yes, I knew it. I told Stephen that you were seeing someone and not telling anyone," she said, leaning back in her chair. "Let me just say I'm thrilled for you," she said. "After the way that awful guy spoke to you, I hope this man is treating you right."

A smile overcame Vanessa and she gazed at her friend. "Thank you. He is. But...when did you sleep with Stephen? When did you feel certain that he was the man for you and you trusted him enough to be completely vulnerable?"

"Uh, it happened pretty quickly. A lot faster than I planned, but our situation was different. We had so little time to get to know one another. We had that Christmas event coming up and I was living with him."

So in less than a month, Brie had slept with Stephen. Why couldn't Vanessa loosen up and give herself to David?

Her friend reached over and placed her hand on hers. "Look, I hadn't lost anyone. I'd dated a whole passel of losers, but I've never lost a husband. So I'm sure this first time with someone other than your husband is going to be hard. But if there is any chance at all of this being a serious, marrying kind of relationship, then relax and do it."

What could she say? She was falling in love with David and he had admitted to falling for her, but after all this time, she still had not committed to sleeping with him. The last time she'd been that vulnerable with someone had been on her wedding night. But now she was older, more experienced, and a better judge of character.

This could be for forever. She wanted to sleep with David, she couldn't wait to feel his arms around her and for their bodies to join. But still she felt anxious. Was it time to get over her fear by jumping into the pool? Time to take that final leap of faith and show David they were a forever kind of love?

"You're right," she said. "This man has been patient and kind and waited for me. It's time I show I trust him and take this step."

Brie glanced at her and smiled. "Oh, girlfriend, you are about to get laid."

Vanessa blushed. "Shh...not so loud."

"If I were you, I'd be shouting it out. This poor man is going to be worn out."

"Brie," she said embarrassed.

"Call me the morning after and give me all the dirty details."

"I will not. That's private."

"Oh, you're going to want to talk to someone. I'm here for you, girlfriend."

CHAPTER 11

*V*anessa stood at the front door to David's house and tried to rid herself of the butter-flies that soared through her body making her tremble. This was so unlike her. She was a strong, vibrant woman capable of living on her own. So why did the thought of sleeping with David terrify her?

All day she thought of their discussion last night. The man admitted to falling in love with her and she confessed the same. So what was she waiting for?

The longer she delayed, the more she could jeopardize this relationship and she didn't want to lose him. Sure, he had said he would wait for her, but why was she holding back? Even Kevin had been frustrated with her for waiting until marriage, but at that time, she had been young and uncertain. Now she was older, but still, she held back.

No one was guaranteed another day, another moment. Both of them were very aware of their limited amount of time on earth.

Taking a deep breath, she rang the bell and he opened the door, pulling her inside and kissing her deeply. When their lips finally broke apart after she moaned, he grinned down at her. "I waited all day to do that."

"You know just what to say," she said, shrugging out of her coat.

"But it's the truth," he said. "How about taco casserole."

"Sounds wonderful," she said, walking into his home. She set her purse down and laid her jacket over the back of a chair.

Glancing around, she was always amazed that a man had kept a home so well. "How was school?"

"Today, I put the team through an intense workout along with a lecture on anyone else caught bullying would be removed from the school baseball roster. We're working hard to win state and get many of them scholarships. I'm not wasting my time with kids who are mean spirited. Hopefully, I sent a powerful message to the other students."

She'd been so proud of the way he didn't let his star players get away with how they'd treated classmates. After two months of dating, she honestly believed David was a good man. A man she hoped to spend a lot of time with.

"Did the one's father back off?"

One of the player's father threatened to have David fired. But her man had stood his ground and refused to be intimidated. Not backing down on his morals made her think even more of David.

"Oh yeah, after I told him to take his complaints to the school board. They shot him down immediately, telling him there was enough documentation to prove his son bullied several students and his actions would not be tolerated on any campus in the district. Amazing how they stood behind me. They refused to let a parent's complaint overrule me."

Relief for David, but also pride that he defended his beliefs and won against the bullying parent over-whelmed Vanessa.

Coming up behind him, she wrapped her arms around his waist. "That's because they knew the baseball coach was right."

He pulled her to his side and the two of them stood in each other's arms as he tossed the salad with one hand. "Here, let me take the other spoon."

Together they stirred the lettuce, laughing at how they didn't want to let go of each other while they did the simplest tasks.

Was this a testament to how it would always be

between them? Passion and desire and happiness flowing around them? What more could she want?

"Okay, I think everything is ready. You pour us some ice water and I'll get the casserole out of the oven," he said.

Thirty minutes later, she helped him clear the table and rinse the dishes, putting them into the dishwasher.

"Are you always this good of a housekeeper?" she asked, surprised at how his house always looked clean. Many men wouldn't care.

"It's just easier to clean it right away. That way I don't have to come back and scrub dried-on food. It takes maybe five minutes."

Vanessa's hands began to sweat and she realized she was walking around aimlessly growing more and more nervous. David, glanced at her and his eyes concerned.

"You okay?" he asked, wiping the last cabinet and coming to her.

"Yes," she whispered with an anxious smile.

What could she say to him? I'm thinking about seducing you tonight and I'm so jumpy because I'm nervous and excited and anxious and so ready for us to do this that I'm a nervous wreck? Yet, you're what I want. Somehow that didn't seem to go together, but yet it did for her.

Finally, she sank down on the couch and he joined her, taking her into his arms. "Do you want to watch some television?"

"No," she said, and he gazed at her, concerned.

"What's going on," he asked.

Licking her lips, she reached up and kissed him hard, her mouth covering his as he took over the kiss, tasting her and showing her how she affected him. Slowly, she pulled back.

Now was the time. If she were going to do this with him tonight, this was the moment and she refused to chicken out. They were adults and they'd waited longer than most people, so tonight was the night.

"All day, my mind has whirled around about what we talked about yesterday," she said, standing and holding out her hand. "You're the only man I picture myself being with. Let's create some memories together."

His mouth dropped open and then he jumped up, took her hand. "Are you sure?"

"Yes," she said and started walking toward his bedroom.

CHAPTER 12

*D*avid wanted to tell her to stop and wait. But couldn't. When was the last time he changed the sheets? Did he have any condoms? Oh goodness, he didn't care. He just wanted this woman in his arms, in his bed, in his life. He longed to wake up with Vanessa by his side every day. Finally, he found a woman to share his days and nights with.

Tomorrow, he would be down at the jewelry store buying her the biggest diamond he could afford and begging her to marry him.

But tonight, they would celebrate his love for her. Show her how much he cared and planned on continuing to care for her. Everything seemed to be happening so quickly, but he knew they were meant for one another.

Following   her   into   the

bedroom, he pulled her into his chest, pressing her to him as he kissed her. Letting his mouth show her the emotions welling up inside him. Knowing, before the night was over, he would whisper to her he loved her.

Gently, with his lips still connected with hers, he led her to where they fell to the bed. As he moved over her fully-clothed body, their lips separated.

"Are you certain," he asked again, knowing this was a huge step for her and giving her the chance to back out.

"Yes," she said, lowering his head to her mouth once again.

Her lips were full and soft and all he wanted was to strip her clothes from her body and let his desire show her what he was feeling.

His hands were shaking as he slowly unbuttoned her blouse. Rising over her, he aided her to a sitting position and slipped her blouse over her head.

In that moment, he noticed her gazing around his bedroom, staring at the photos on the wall, on his dresser. They had been there since Becky's illness and he had forgotten all about them. In his grief, he never cleansed his home of Becky's presence.

The desire shining from her sapphire eyes died, replaced with panic that reflected in her gaze.

"Vanessa?" he asked feeling her tense in his arms.

At first, she didn't respond, but tears welled up in her eyes. She was going to run. Already he sensed the change in her feelings.

"What's wrong?" he asked, pausing, giving her a chance to tell him.

Gazing around the room she stared. "The photos. So many, many pictures of the two of you."

What had he been thinking? Obviously, his mind no longer saw the pictures and until now, he never considered how it would look to someone else.

Suddenly she grabbed her shirt and yanked it over her body. "I can't do this. This room...you're not ready."

"Vanessa," he repeated softly trying to calm her. "It doesn't mean anything."

She turned on him and he could see that was the wrong thing to say. "What do you mean it doesn't mean anything. Look around. All I see are photos of your dead wife everywhere. Images of the two of you together. This doesn't feel right. Do you still love her?"

Shocked, he couldn't respond as he saw for the first time in years what she was seeing.

Jumping up, she jerked her shoes on and hurried out of the room.

He ran after her realizing he was a damn fool.

"Vanessa," he called, hurrying after her. "Stop and let's talk about this."

Grabbing her coat and purse, she fled to the door. "I can't. I've got to get out of here."

"Please stop," he said.

"Goodbye, David," she said and walked out the door.

Why did that sound so final?

How could he be so stupid? The pictures of him and Becky in their bedroom were put there years ago. Many he added when she became so deathly ill, hoping to encourage and give her strength during those difficult days. But they had been there so long, he never thought about them, never considering how it must appear to Vanessa.

Yes, he still loved Becky. He always would, but she was gone and now he also loved Vanessa.

He only prayed those images hadn't ended it with the woman he so desperately wanted to create a life with.

CHAPTER 13

*D*riving home, Vanessa cried all the way, wiping at the tears to clear her vision. After Kevin died, in the middle of the night, she made the decision to move. There were too many memories in the old place they shared.

At the new place, she decided not to put up pictures of the two of them together. Looking at the face of the man she loved while trying to get over him hadn't been possible. So she left the photos packed in a box in the attic.

Lying there in David's bed, seeing photos of him and Becky everywhere seemed wrong. Almost like she was committing adultery with a married man. An uneasy guilt had come over her, and as crazy as it sounded, she felt like she'd been a mistress sleeping in another woman's bed.

With the wedding, vacation, and family photos, his bedroom had the appearance of a shrine to his dead wife. How could she give herself to David with images of him and Becky staring down as she and David committed the most intimate act on earth?

Right now distance was needed to decide if she wanted to continue dating. Regardless of what he said, was this a warning sign he wasn't ready for a commitment? Was he still dealing with grief for the woman he once loved?

Maybe she should have stayed and talked to him about her feelings, but the urge to get far from that room with another woman's stamp on it overwhelmed her. She needed time to think about her own reaction. Determine if David was really over his wife, and if so, why did images of the two of them occupy so much space in that room? Why?

What kind of man expected her to relax and let him make love to her under the watchful eyes of his late wife?

Tears flowed unchecked down her cheeks. This evening, when she went to David's house, she imagined a new beginning for both of them. The possibility of happiness once again. But now--now all of her confidence in the two of them seemed empty.

The only certainty was the fact that she was in love with a man who still loved his dead wife.

And she refused to live in the shadows of another woman living or dead. After everything she went through with the death of Kevin, she deserved more.

CHAPTER 14

*D*avid went into his room and glanced around at the photos on the wall, the dresser, the nightstand. They were everywhere. For a smart man, tonight he'd been dumber than a pile of rocks. A gripping pain in his chest ached at the loss of Vanessa and he prayed it was only temporary.

The pictures from the past were a reflection of a time in his life when he'd been happy. But Becky was gone and he had found a wonderful woman. The opportunity to experience love once again. Sure, he would always love Becky, but he also loved Vanessa and this was their moment. Becky would want that for him.

These pictures had been up so long, he failed to see them any longer. They were ornaments from a life he no longer had that he never removed. What kind of idiot left photos of his first wife out while trying to seduce his second? Nothing would ever bring Becky back, and now it was time to begin again with a new love.

In the garage, he located a plastic box and carried it into the room. Time to put away the past, something he should have done years ago.

Slowly he took down the pictures, each one a precious memory of his previous life. By the time he finished, he knew he wanted to replace those photos with new, happy memories of him and Vanessa.

His time with Becky was at an end and he hoped he could repair the damage with Vanessa. Tomorrow after school, he would attempt to make things right. But would she give him a second chance to prove his love?

CHAPTER 15

The next day, the sun had already set and the idea of going home to a dark, empty house where the only thing waiting for her was loneliness didn't appeal. Compelled to take a walk, she found herself at the park.

Darkness shrouded the area except for the Cupid statue bathed in light. Taking a seat on the park bench, she listened to the night sounds, not afraid, but at peace. Almost comforted by the boy in a diaper. No, she didn't expect to see Kevin here again; he was gone.

While she never sought to replace him, she dreamed of having a second chance at love. And she thought she would with David. Last night, doubt and confusion about him being over his wife overwhelmed her as she ran out the door.

Never would she expect him to forget her, just like

she would always remember Kevin. A piece of her heart belonged to Kevin, but she also wanted to give the rest of her heart to a living, breathing man who loved her.

Now, she was questioning if he was ready. Maybe it had been a coincidence, but snapshots of all those happy moments of the two of them together left her feeling like an outsider. Not a place she could be her most vulnerable in - another woman's bedroom.

With a sigh, she glanced up at the God of Love. Yes, she loved David. She'd fallen in love with his kind spirit and the way he made her laugh and try new things. In the last two months, she had more fun and started to believe they would make each other very happy.

The sound of footsteps sent a tremor of fear through her. Sure, this was Cupid, Texas, small-town America where nothing bad happened, but that didn't mean it couldn't be a first.

David suddenly burst into the clearing. "There you are. I've been looking everywhere for you. You're not answering your cell phone."

Though she didn't want to feel anything, excitement pulsed through her veins at the sight of his handsome face. No, if he wasn't ready, she couldn't be in love with him, but that emotion didn't just turn off. It filled her heart and flowed through her veins.

"It died," she said, trying to quell the emotions rocking her. "It's charging in the car."

His eyes widened and he shook his head. "You came out here to the park alone without it?"

When he said it that way, not having her phone did sound rather stupid. "Until now, I didn't worry."

"Well, I was," he said running his hand through his hair. He sank down next to her. "Can we talk about last night?"

This would be her chance to say goodbye. Her opportunity to tell him he wasn't ready. That all those snapshots revealed his true feelings.

Nodding, she knew she had to speak. "I'm sorry, I d—

"

Holding up his hand, he stopped her. "You have nothing to be sorry about. As you can tell, no other woman has entered my bedroom. Those pictures were all hung when Becky was alive. After she passed, I never thought to change anything. The entire house is just like she left it, including the bedroom."

That's why the house was perfectly decorated. She wasn't seeing what he'd done, but rather what Becky had done to the home.

With a sigh, he picked up her hand. "When she was seriously ill, I added more pictures of us, hoping they would give her strength and remind her to fight even harder to stay here with me. But it wasn't meant to be. Then after she was gone, I just never removed them. When I enter the room, I don't even see them."

That must be true. Because why would he have left

them there if he wanted her to sleep with him? But did he understand how those photos made her feel?

"Seeing those snapshots, I felt like an interloper stealing another woman's man. The images made giving myself to you impossible. If you still grieve for her, this is not going to work. If we're going to be together, I can't compete with your dead wife for your affection."

If she had to, she would walk away from David and once again, learn to live alone. As a strong woman, she was capable of being on her own, but she would so much rather be with him.

"Understood and I agree. Those pictures have been there so long, I don't see them. They're gone. Packed them all and moved them to the attic."

Pausing, he glanced down before he looked into her eyes.

"Last night, you asked me if I still loved Becky and I didn't answer. No matter what, I will always love and have a special place in my heart for her. But she's gone and I have the opportunity to have happiness with you. She would want that for me. So yes, I still love her, but I also love you."

Dropping down from the bench, he landed on one knee and her heart slammed in her chest, tears welling up in her eyes.

"We were thrown together at a party, two strangers, each seeking what we'd lost. With you, I found the love missing in my life. You make me a better man. You challenge and keep me honest. For that and many more reasons, I love you and want to share everything with you. Have babies, grand babies, and die whispering your name on my lips. Please do me the honor of being my wife."

Vanessa thought about the two of them, they were good for each other. And his explanation for the pictures fit him and made perfect sense. If he loved her half as much as she loved him, they could be happy. "Yes, David, I'll marry you."

Standing, he pulled her into his arms and kissed her with a long slow kiss that had her senses rattled from the desire that swept over her. Breaking apart, he stared down in her eyes.

"Since you and Kevin never lived in your home, maybe we should live there."

Smiling up at him, contentment filled her knowing she wouldn't lose the property on the river. David was exactly what the house needed, a strong man to make it a home. Together, the place would become theirs. "That pleases me so much. What if we had a wall where we put pictures of Becky and Kevin. They were a big part of our lives and this way we show respect to them."

Squeezing her tightly, he said, "I like that idea."

Pulling his phone out of his pocket, he leaned his head against hers. "Smile."

With a click, he took the photo and she stared at him questioning. "Our home should be decorated with our pictures. This one is for us to show our children, the night we became engaged. More than anything, I want photos of our wedding day. The sooner, the better. To make you feel more comfortable, we're going to wait until we're married to consummate our marriage."

Staring up at the man she loved, her heart swelled at his willingness to wait for her. How many men would be so thoughtful? And the photo for the children brought tears to her eyes.

"Thank you," she said, squeezing him tightly. "David, I love you."

"I love you," he said and they walked out of the park together.

In the background, neither saw the two shimmering figures.

"Looks like she found love again," the spirit said.

"Yes, thank you, Uncle. I didn't want her to be alone."

CHAPTER 16

*T*hree weeks later, Vanessa invited all her friends over for a party. Spring was in the air and David and she decided to make the occasion special. A surprise wedding. Only four people were told about the event: Brie and Stephen and David's parents. Brie was the maid of honor and Stephen seated the stunned guests as they arrived.

From the upstairs window, Vanessa watched as their friends and family sat whispering in shock, wondering who the lucky man was.

Just before the music began, David walked downstairs along with his father as the guests clapped with glee. Now everyone would learn that the horrible Valentine's celebration where they first met had been an act. At the sound of the music, Brie turned to Vanessa and hugged her.

"Here's to happily ever after," she said.

"Thanks, Brie."

This moment, she wanted to remember everything. Soaking in this special day, she stared as her friend walked down the stairs to the arch they had decorated in the backyard.

Vanessa walked toward her new love. Her eyes met David's and she smiled with joy. Today their life together began and she could hardly wait.

I HAD no intention of writing Vanessa's story, but something pulled at me that she needed her happily ever after and then it become one of my favorites. This was supposed to be the last book in this series, but then I had another crazy idea. Keep reading for a sneak preview of Cupid Charmer.

"SO THE CHARMER is ready to settle down," Max Vandenberg, retired football star and resident of Cupid, Texas, said sipping his beer.

Sitting across from him at Valentino's Bar, the only honky-tonk in town, Aaron Johnson laughed at the nickname the papers had labeled him with.

A country song about losing love and heartache

played on the jukebox while couples danced. Some men hung out in the back, playing pool while others sat farther from the noisy talking.

"I'm not a charmer. More like lady bait. I'm sick and tired of women chasing me to learn the only thing they're interested in is my cash."

The software app he created in college made him a billionaire when he couldn't buy a date. Now, he couldn't rid himself of the female leeches. He had more money than he would ever need, and that wealth was the very reason he returned to Cupid.

That and a good-looking brunette he remembered from high school and thought of often. Especially after her disastrous attempt to marry his once best friend, Jason Walker. Keyword - once.

"Understand, man," Max said. "Had that problem when I played professional ball. Once they learned you were a football player, they thought you were rich and famous and wanted to tap into that golden river."

For years, Aaron tried dating, and it seemed he compared every woman to a certain girl here in town that he couldn't forget.

"They're all fakes, and every time I thought I'd found someone, they would show their true side. Quickly, I realized all they wanted was what my money afforded them." Shaking his head, he sighed. "Man, I want to get married and have a couple of kids. But I'm not going to tie myself to a fake Barbie doll."

The business was doing well enough, it almost ran itself, and now he wanted to expand and do some charity work. Find the right woman, have two point five children and enjoy life.

Instead, he had women who wouldn't have considered him in college throwing themselves at him. Not that he was bad looking, but before, he didn't meet their criteria, and now his money did.

With a groan, Max laughed. "Those days were some crazy days and I don't envy you one bit."

The two men had been friends since high school, and they were both back in the small Texas town where Aaron had a plan for the place he grew up. A chance to give back to the community. "You're happily married to Meghan. How did you two get back together? When we left for college, the two of you weren't even speaking."

His friend laughed. "She did the Cupid dance one night and I just happened to be driving by when I saw Meghan running down the street naked. Max smiled and shook his head. "My wife sprinting bare ass down the road is not a sight you forget."

The town had a superstition. Dance naked around the Cupid statue at midnight, chanting some hocus pocus, and the first person you saw was your true love. Every year, there was talk of taking down the statue of the God of Love in the park.

The church ladies wanted the blasphemous sculpture that led people to love removed. Every year, another group in town saved the stone effigy the town's founder erected.

"Please tell me you don't believe that nonsense," Aaron said, gazing in surprise at Max.

"Yes, I do. Not only did Meghan do it, but her friends Taylor and Kelsey, both met and married the first men they ran into that night. Kelsey's brothers, Randy, Kyle, and Drew Lawrence all met their wives, doing the Cupid dance."

"No way," Aaron responded. In his logical computing mind, that didn't make a bit of sense. "That's all superstition. It's bullshit."

"And it works," Max said, glancing at his watch. "Since tonight is Valentine's, you might want to consider trying the Cupid dance. I could be your backup."

Still not really believing in this superstition, he stared at Max. "How come you're out with me, a single guy on Valentine's Day? Why aren't you with your wife and kids?"

Tonight he should be with his wife, not here with Aaron.

"The boys are sick, so we're celebrating this weekend. Don't worry, I'm taking home Meghan a box of chocolates and saying thank you for letting me hang out with you. This is a luxury. With two kids, there aren't many nights I'm able to go out alone. Meghan will be rewarded with a Mother's day off once the boys are well."

Earlier in the evening, Max had shown him pictures of his boys, and Aaron thought how wonderful to raise children with someone you loved. There must've been difficult times, but still, the thought left him envious. This was what he wanted. What he needed, but at the moment, there was no one in the picture.

A sigh escaped Aaron as he sipped on his beer. "Man, I'm jealous of your life. You and Meghan appear to have it all."

Max smiled. "It wasn't always this way. We went through a pretty rough patch, but we're happy and my family means everything to me. Dance naked around the statue and it's true you could have what we have."

The idea was preposterous. Sure, he knew people in town swore by the statue, but dancing naked didn't seem logical or rational or anything an intellectual man would do.

"Do you miss the women pursuing you?"

Max almost spewed his beer. "Oh hell, no. Just like you, all the drama got old," Max told him. "The Charmer needs to find himself a woman and settle down. And I know how he can find her."

As Max glanced at his wrist again. "We've got about twenty minutes before the bell tolls midnight. Tonight might be the night you finally meet the woman of your dreams."

Aaron's insides tightened, especially his groin as his thoughts turned to the one woman he once wanted years ago. "Or I could freeze my nuts off and be arrested for indecent exposure."

With a quick nod, Max smiled. "Grab the check. Let's go so you can do the Cupid dance."

With every fiber of his being screaming no, Aaron knew something needed to change. The last three years since college had been nothing but one phony woman after another. Maybe it was time to try something different. Maybe the alcohol was talking.

"All right, I hope I don't regret this ridiculous idea. I hope I don't find myself looking out from behind bars tonight."

"Come on, Cupid Charmer. True love awaits."

Available at all Major Retailers!

PLEASE LEAVE A REVIEW

Did you enjoy the book? Reviews help authors. I would appreciate you posting a review everywhere

Follow Sylvia on Facebook.

Sign up for my new book alert at www. SylviaMcDaniel.com **and receive a complimentary book.**

Nothing says bad judgement like trying to prove a superstition true...

After returning to her hometown, Taylor Braxton, along with a few adventurous girlfriends, decides to test the Cupid superstition at midnight on Valentine's Day. After all, Taylor reasons, what is the worst thing that can happen – the superstition of finding her true love might come true?

Sheriff Ryan Jones is used to getting calls about people dancing around the downtown fountain. When you live in Cupid, Texas, there were always some residents who believed if you dance naked around the fountain, you were guaranteed to find your true love. What he doesn't expect is to find the lovely, but spirited Taylor Braxton confronting him at midnight – sans clothing. Unfortunately, a long-held promise and his badge stand between him and what he wants – Taylor.

Will the Cupid Superstition help Taylor and Ryan overcome the past and take a chance on love again? Or will a promise he made to her best friend—his ex, and his career, deflect Cupid's arrow?

Available at Your Favorite Retailer!

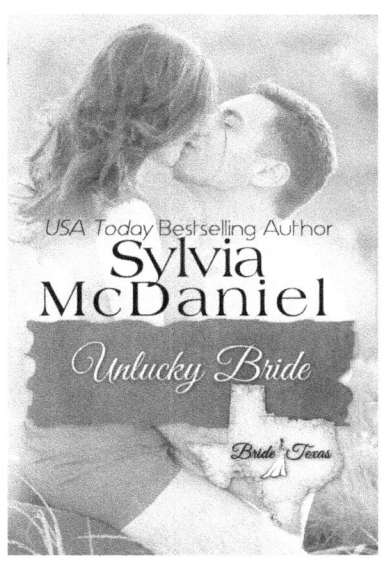

Chapter One

Cupid, Texas

"Laney Baxter, if you have reservations, back out now," Ally, her best friend and bridesmaid said. "Your son doesn't need a father that badly."

Reaching up, Laney touched the gold heart necklace around her neck. Maybe not, but the boy was growing from toddler to little boy, and her son would do better with the influence of a strong man.

Deliberately, she kept her son's father's identity a secret. No one needed to know, not her family, her friends, or even her best friend. For one thing, it would lead to all kinds of questions she was too embarrassed to explain. Especially to her parents.

"Not really reservations. Roger is just not who I envisioned marrying," Laney admitted, not willing to concede she dreamed of walking down the aisle with Ally's brother Chase.

"Do you love him? Please tell me you are not shackling yourself to a man you don't care about."

"Of course, I love Roger. He's a good man. But I expected I would be more excited about tomorrow," she confessed.

Roger was everything she could want. Patient and kind, he agreed to wait to consummate their relationship. After the pee stick changed color, she made the decision that until a ring graced her left finger and a license proclaimed her his wife, there would be no sharing her bed. What was that old saying?

Once burned, twice shy.

"Don't you think your lack of excitement is telling?"

Flipping her shoulder length brown hair back, she shook her head. "After being heartbroken by Trenton's dad, the disappearance of Jim, nothing about love excites me anymore. My lack of excitement is my attempt to guard my heart."

After an unplanned pregnancy and an abandoned engagement, when it came to men, caution was best.

Ally tossed back her glass of wine. "In high school, you were always the life of the party. Creating more mischief than any of the other girls we hung with. And yet, here you are the night before your big day holed up with me in The Cupid Love Nest bed and breakfast. Not even a bachelorette night on the town. We should be down at Valentino's bar drinking champagne and being toasted."

With a shrug, she said, "I'm a parent now. My son is my first priority."

The idea of getting drunk wasn't appealing. She only planned on marrying once and a clear head was optimal when she took her vows. What if Trenton became sick or called for her? He didn't need an out of control mother.

"Lord, I never realized how much having a child could change a person."

A laugh came from Laney's lips as she considered how her life had changed since Trenton arrived. At first, she'd been distraught over having a child. Now, Trenton was a blessing. When he grinned and held up his arms, her heart clenched with love for her little man. Forsaking her single lifestyle was easy.

Her only regret was his father.

Barely three years of age, Trenton's birth transformed her world for the better.

"Your mom is keeping him while you two go off on your honeymoon?"

"No honeymoon. We're spending the night in Fort Worth, and Sunday, we'll come back here. Monday, I move into his apartment," she said, thinking how odd it would be to leave her family home.

Living with them for twenty-four years was longer than she planned. After her parents learned of her pregnancy, they encouraged and helped her finish college while watching their grandson.

Because of their generosity, she had her bachelor's degree in elementary education. Leaving Trenton with her mother every day while she attended school, eased her mind that her son was looked after and so very loved.

Now, the time had come to grow up and face her responsibilities with a new husband.

Sipping the last of her bubbly, she thought back to that one night, when minus her panties, she let down her guard.

The superstition of dancing naked around the Cupid statue in the town square said the next person you met should be your true love. The consequences of her jaunt around that piece of rock appeared nine months later with the delivery of her beautiful baby boy.

Shame, his father didn't have the courage to listen to her when she tried to tell him the results of their one night together where even a condom didn't stop her from getting pregnant. Instead, he'd been too busy going off to graduate school than to learn they were expecting.

One day when Trenton was old enough, they would have a long talk about his father. It would be hard to keep the bitterness from her voice and the anger from her words. His father followed his dreams while she had their child.

"If you decide against this wedding, you're welcome to escape to the family cabin on the banks of the Leon River right outside Bride, Texas. That crazy little town started by the jilted bride."

"A jilted bride started that hole in the wall?"

"Yes, she was stood up by her fiancé and she created a life for herself right there. A beautiful story to remind brides that sometimes there is something better coming along," Ally said, smiling. "It's one of the reasons I like it there."

"Thank you, but I won't need a place. I'm getting married in twenty-four hours."

"Well, here's the key to the cabin," Ally said, dangling the metal like a temptation. "I'll carry it in my bouquet, just in case."

Laney giggled. "Thanks, but next week, I'll be moving into Roger's apartment as his wife and he as Trenton's father."

Ally took a deep sigh and released it. "You realize you have the worst luck with guys. What makes you think marriage will be any better?"

"Yes, I agree I'm unlucky when it comes to men," she said, her eyes blinking with unshed tears.

This was her second endeavor at standing before a preacher and saying vows. Not long after the birth of

Trenton, she met Jim who asked her to marry him, only six weeks before the ceremony, he walked away. Disappeared without a call, without a trace.

An unplanned pregnancy, a broken engagement, and now the night before her big day, she had jitters. Nothing more than nerves.

Ally shook her head. "Don't know why, I always thought you would wed Chase. Ever since my brother picked you up that night we dared you to dance in the buff around Cupid, I pictured the two of you together."

"Sometimes even Cupid gets it wrong," she said, knowing she thought she would wed him as well.

Laney stood in the vestibule of the church, in her white satin dress and veil waiting for the wedding march to begin. Doubts assailed her like hail in a Texas thunderstorm. Just like Ally had the night before, she questioned if she should marry Roger.

A gorgeous, rock-solid man who had a great job, supported her, treated her special, kissed well...*but not as earth moving like the man who broke your heart*, her conscious reminded her.

Reaching up, she touched the gold heart necklace, still wondering who had sent her the jewelry. Not long after she did the Cupid dance, it arrived in an unmarked box. No return address, no name, nothing. Now, she considered it her lucky charm.

"Are you certain?" her father asked. "It's not too late to back out."

"Let's go, Daddy," she said, refusing to let her apprehension overcome her. "He's a good man."

"Yes, he is," her father replied. "Is he the right man for my daughter?"

"Come on, Dad. They're waiting," she said, plastering a smile on her face, not answering. That would be a long discussion. One they didn't have time for.

"Okay, let's go," he said and patted her on the hand.

Walking down the aisle, she barely glanced at the people who were seated. Her eyes were on the man she was about to commit her life to, hoping she was making the right choice.

As she neared Roger, she noticed he appeared anxious. Sweat beaded on his forehead. Of course, he was nervous. They were making a lifetime commitment today. A major life event.

Smiling, she tried to reassure him as she approached the altar.

"Who gives this woman away?"

"Her mother and I," her father said, handing her off to Roger. Placing her hand in his, she gave a quick, reassuring squeeze.

The pastor looked out at the people gathered for the ceremony. "Should there be anyone who has cause why this couple should not be united in holy matrimony, please say so now."

The door of the church slammed open and the sound of high-heels running down the aisle had her frowning as she watched Roger's eyes widened, his mouth dropped open, and she knew. Like a bolt of lightning, she just knew...

The color faded from her fiancé's face as he gasped, and her stomach tightened. Taking a deep breath, she fortified herself for the bad news. Unlucky again.

"Excuse me, but this man is married," a shrill voice sounded as their friends and family mumbled to each other.

A short woman with bottled-blonde hair and a set of decorated designer boobs displayed down to the top of her nipples, stood waving a piece of paper, a hefty rock on her left hand. "This is a copy of the marriage license. I have a ring on my finger and our wedding photo."

Reaching for her beacon of hope, Laney's fingers flew to the golden heart necklace around her throat.

Relief seemed to flood Laney and the look of horror on Roger's face made her burst out laughing. From the distress etched on his face, she grasped the woman's claim was true. Anger flooded her body like a Texas downpour racing through the streets. The man who supposedly loved her let her make a complete fool of herself.

"You low-life jerk," she said low enough for only his ears. "You're married. When were you going to tell me?"

"No, no," he cried as she walked back down the petal covered carpet, her satin skirt swishing, determination in every step to elude this fiasco.

"The marriage is not real. It happened in Vegas," Roger howled. "Stop, Laney, stop."

"Oh, yes, it did," the woman said. "We met, spent the night together, and woke up the next morning in wedded bliss. After I went to get coffee, you left before we talked about where we're going to live."

"That was fake," he exclaimed.

"Oh no, baby. This sealed document is as real as it gets. You belong to me."

Nearing the heavily made-up woman, Laney sensed her parents surrounding her, her precious son in her mother's arms. The touch of her father's hand at her elbow, guiding her around the circus she could see unfolding there in the church, was comforting.

Roger begged his new wife to stop as she shoved the paper that shackled him to the platinum bombshell in his face. "Honey, I'm so glad I showed up. Bigamy is against the law."

"Right now, jail would be better than the hell I'm living."

The vulgar woman laughed. "That's not what you said in bed the other night."

Hurrying past the unfolding chaos, a loud scuffling

noise came from behind. Looking over her shoulder to see Roger sprawled in the aisle, a satisfied look of retaliation spread on her grandmother's face.

Granny could be deadly with her cane, buying Laney time to escape the auditorium. Smiling at the woman she loved, she gave her a thumbs up.

Laney hurried out the chapel. Funny, she wasn't crying. She wasn't even sad. Actually, she felt at peace. As they reached the vestibule, she turned to her mother and took her son from her arms.

"What are you doing?" her mother asked, emerald eyes filled with tears.

"I'm leaving town for a little while," she said, knowing instinctively this was what she should do. Hide out from the drama swirling around her and Roger. Getting away was the only reason she would have any serenity. Moving as swift as her taffeta skirt would allow, she made her way past the stunned wedding planner.

"Let me keep Trenton," her mother said, running after her.

"Thank you, Mom, but I need my son. Give me a chance to get away, and I promise, I'll call you later. At the moment, I must leave."

The impulse to race as fast as she could from the scene of her latest disaster sped through her like the adrenaline of running. The fight or flight urge was all flight. The flaxen-haired sex kitten could have Roger.

In a fog, she entered the bride's room, picked up the overnight bag. Trenton would need more clothes in a few days or a washing machine would work, but she didn't care. Thank goodness, her suitcase was already in the trunk of her car.

Soon as she could grab the rest of her stuff, she would run out the building, though she had no plan where she would go.

Following behind her into the suite, her mother's face was streaked with tears. A distressed frown crinkled her father's forehead as he tried to comfort her mother while he scrutinized his daughter.

"Mom, I'm all right. Let me slip away so Roger can't reach me. The wedding was ruined by his lovely new wife and I hope they're very unhappy together."

"Your mother stopped me from punching him," her father said. "I wanted to deck him."

"Thank you," she said, her heart aching for the hurt her parents were feeling as she reached over and kissed them each on the cheek. Just then, she heard Roger's voice yelling for her at the top of his lungs.

"Mom, Dad, I'm sorry, I've got to get out of here. Trust me, I'm okay, but I don't want to speak to him."

Reaching into his pocket, her father pulled out a wad of cash. "In case you need something. Don't forget to call. We'll be waiting to hear from you."

"As soon as we arrive," she said and squeezed her mother's arm.

"Be careful," her mother said and her father wrapped her in his arms.

Picking up her bags, Laney rushed down the hall to the chapel exit, her wedding dress swishing. If only she had time to change clothes. At the door, she saw Ally leaning against the frame, twirling a key.

"Told you so," she said and handed her the shining metal.

"I don't..." The cabin was the perfect place. A small little house tucked on the river, away from town, away from everyone until the melodramatics died down. The kind of place to disappear for a while. Soak up the sun and rest.

"The weather is supposed to become nasty later today, so be watchful. Call me if you have any trouble," Ally said. "Even if you want a little company."

Laney gave her an awkward hug. "This is why I love you. Trenton and I will enjoy the solitude and the quiet."

When the dust settled, she would tell Ally how right she was about her luck with men, but right now, she had to leave or face Roger.

"Now, go. Somehow a reporter showed up and is wanting to do a story on the Unlucky Bride. An interview you don't want to give."

A sarcastic laugh bubbled up from within her. "Why do I have the worst luck when it comes to men?" A glance at her son and her heart swelled with love. "Except that one time I got you, buddy."

"Go," Ally commanded. "And be careful of the—"

Suddenly a flash bulb went off in her face. Ducking her son's head, she ran to her car - all decorated with streamers announcing they were man and wife.

A curse slipped from her lips.

"No, Mommy, bad word," Trenton told her.

"You're right, son. Mommy won't say it again," she promised.

"Where's Roger?" he asked.

"Gone for good," she said and buckled him in his seat.

Starting the car, she drove out of the parking lot, prophylactics flying from her grill, tin cans bouncing behind her, streamers proclaiming just married. More like, publicly dumped.

Thunder rumbled, the house shuddering as Chase Hamilton stared out the window at the rain streaming from the sky. Why in the hell had he come here to this little cabin in the middle of godforsaken nowhere?

Growing up in Cupid, Texas, where people danced naked around a boy in a diaper sculpture to find their true love, he was shocked to learn how a jilted woman started this beautiful community. His parents' weekend getaway sat about a hundred feet from the Leon River, right outside Bride, Texas - where jilted women sought answers to their love life.

What about cheated on men? Where did they go?

To a home along the Leon River to heal. Two broken ribs, a black eye, and a bruised heart. In an irresponsible act of rage, he threw the first punch, creating a scene and barely escaping arrest. All because Cissy, who he enjoyed dating, didn't believe in monogamy. Now, he asked himself, had she been worth all the pain and anger.

Hell, no.

Limping away from the window, he sank back onto the couch, placing the ice pack on his bruised body. Staring at the blank screen of the television, he pondered his life, taking stock of where to go from here.

"Fighting is for losers," he said out loud, his brain agreeing with him. His heart saying *come on, you'd punch the jerk again.*

You don't hit women, children, or animals and the man had done two out of three in front of Chase causing him to lose his meager self-control.

Sadly, Cissy's dramatics outweighed the positives and left him reeling. In the end, she'd chosen the muscled brute over Chase, regardless that the wrestler kicked her dog and slapped her beautiful face.

That kind of crazy, he didn't need - though until then, she seemed so perfect.

Headlights flashed through the darkened room and

slowly he rose to his feet. Who could be driving out here in this awful weather? No one knew he had escaped here to lick his wounds and mend in private.

A small Honda splashed on the dirt drive leading to the house. What were they doing coming out here now?

The car stopped and a woman opened the car door and stepped out. Her head bent to avoid the slashing rain drops as she reached inside the backseat of the car. As the woman turned and faced him, his chest tightened, his stomach churned, and he couldn't believe his eyes.

Laney Baxter in a long, lace wedding dress dashed through the puddles running toward the cabin, a little boy in her arms. The memory of their one night together slammed into his gut, wrenching his very soul and he groaned. Not what his recovery needed.

Stepping under the awning, she set the child down and he heard the key in the lock. Chase yanked the door open and she jumped back, her eyes wide with fright.

"Chase," she said in shock, her emerald eyes widening. How he loved gazing into her eyes, feeling like he'd come home.

Shaking his head, he confirmed his eyes weren't betraying him, she was indeed wearing a wedding gown.

"Where's the groom?"

"Left him at church," she said, emptying water out of her shoes.

"What the hell are you doing here? Where did you get a key?"

"Ally told me I could use the cabin for a while."

"Well, she's wrong. You've got to leave."

Laney reached up and ran her hand through her wet hair and glanced down at her son who stared up at her in confusion. "Momma?"

"Ally didn't tell me you would be here. I'm sorry," she said. "I thought I would be alone."

"She doesn't know I'm here. No one knows and I want to keep it that way."

"Little late for that," she said. "When I return, she's going to want to know why."

The little boy tugged on the tulle of her gown and Chase wondered what happened that she came here and not on her fabulous honeymoon.

"Momma," he said a little louder.

How could a man or a woman hit a child or an animal? Yes, he'd been wrong to stoop to the man's level, and yes, he was paying the price for his rage. When his fist connected with the tough wrestler's cheek, the explosion of flesh and bone felt good, until his retaliation shot landed in Chase's ribs.

Never one to wrestle and throw a punch quickly, he had been no match against the professional.

Glancing down at the child, the vision of a screaming toddler invading his personal space made his decision. They had to leave.

"Tell her you couldn't reach the house. Tell her anything. But you can't stay here."

"You're going to send us back out into the storm," she said, her eyes narrowing.

The two of them shared one magical night of being together, and right now, his heart was dealing with his latest love disaster leaving him vulnerable. Too vulnerable to the charms of Laney. Even in her wet, muddied, now ruined, wedding dress, her mahogany hair falling around her shoulders, she looked stunning.

Whatever happened, the man had been a fool to let her go, and Chase couldn't be around her. Not now, not even with a downpour raging outside. She was hurricane force winds of danger compared to cold front Cissy.

"Momma, I need to go potty," the little boy said impatiently. "Now."

"Can my son at least use your restroom before we go back out into the storm?"

A twinge of guilt gripped him and his logical side reminded him of the dangers.

"Of course," he said. He wasn't a complete monster. Just a man confused and hurt and trying to recover.

Taking the boy by the hand, she led him into the living area and straight to the bathroom. In fewer than five minutes, they returned.

"Come on, son, let's go."

"We're not staying?"

"No, we're not," she said defiantly and walked out the door without saying goodbye. "Men are such dicks."

Peering out at the pouring rain, he watched from the door as she loaded the little boy into the child seat in the back of the car. Regret ate at his insides, he should stop her. The thought of a kid running through the house, making noise and the constant presence of Laney kept his lips shut.

Climbing into the car, she started the vehicle and backed away.

Chase closed the door, the silence eating at him. He should have let her stay. Frustrated, but thinking he'd been heartless, he yanked open the door to stop her. Running into the rain after her, to keep her from going, all he saw were tail lights going down the long drive.

One minute, he was trying to save someone and getting injured in the process, and the next, he was sending a woman and child out in a storm. Maybe she was right. Maybe he was just as much of a dick as Cissy's new love.

Available at Your Favorite Retailer

Contemporary Romance
Burnett Brides Contemporary Times

Travis

Tanner

Tucker

Joshua

Jacob

Justin

Return to Cupid, Texas

Cupid Stupid

Cupid Scores

Cupid's Dance

Cupid Help Me!

Cupid Cures

**Cupid's Heart

Cupid Santa

**Cupid Second Chance

Cupid Charmer

Cupid Crazy

Cupid's Bachelorette

Cupid Games

Return to Cupid Box Set Books 1-3

Cupid Help Me Box Set Books 4-6

**The Unlucky Bride

Contemporary Romance
My Sister's Boyfriend
The Wanted Bride
The Reluctant Santa
The Relationship Coach
Secrets, Lies, & Online Dating

Bride, Texas Multi-Author Series
**The Unlucky Bride

Lipstick and Lead 2.0
Nailing the Hit Man
Nailing the Billionaire
Nailing the Single Dad

Secrets of Mustang Island
Secrets of a Summer Place
Secrets of a Runaway Bride
Secrets From the Past

The Langley Legacy
Collin's Challenge

Short Sexy Reads
Racy Reunions Series
Paying For the Past
Her Christmas Lie
Cupid's Revenge

Western Historicals
A Hero's Heart
Second Chance Cowboy
Ethan

American Brides
**Katie: Bride of Virginia

Angel Creek Christmas Brides
Charity
Ginger
Minnie
Cora

The Burnett Brides Series
The Rancher Takes A Bride
The Outlaw Takes A Bride
The Marshal Takes A Bride
The Christmas Bride
Boxed Set

Lipstick and Lead Series
Desperate
Deadly
Dangerous
Daring
**Determined
Deceived

Defiant

Devious

Lipstick and Lead Box Set Books 1-4

**Quinlan's Quest

Mail Order Bride Tales

**A Brother's Betrayal

**Pearl

**Ace's Bride

Scandalous Suffragettes of the West

**Abigail

Bella

Mistletoe Scandal

Southern Historical Romance

A Scarlet Bride

Charity

The Cuvier Women

Wronged

Betrayed

Beguiled

Boxed Set

** Denotes a sweet book.

Want to learn about my new releases before anyone else? Sign up for my New Book Alert and receive a free book.

USA Today Best-selling author, Sylvia McDaniel obviously has too much time on her hands. With over eighty western historical and contemporary romance novels, she spends most days torturing her characters. Bad boys deserve punishment and even good girls get into trouble. Always looking for the next plot twist, she's known for her sweet, funny, family-oriented romances.

Married to her best friend for over twenty-five years, they recently moved to the state of Colorado where they like to hike, and enjoy the beauty of the forest behind their home with their spoiled dachshund Zeus. (He has his own column in her newsletter.)

Their grown son, still lives in Texas. An avid football watcher, she loves the Broncos and the Cowboys, especially when they're winning.

www.SylviaMcDaniel.com
Sylvia@SylviaMcDaniel.com
The End!